Otto Weiss And God Saw That It Was Bad

K narozeninám 1943
věnují
Ota a Helga

Terezín, 22. června

Otto Weiss

And God Saw That It Was Bad
A Story from the Terezín Ghetto

Illustrations: Helga Weissová-Hošková

Yad Vashem • Jerusalem
The International Institute for Holocaust Research

Otto Weiss
I viděl bůh, že je to špatné
Terezínská provídka

All illustrations created by Ms. Helga Weissová-Hošková
at the age of 13

Translated from the Czech: Iris Urwin
Academic Editor: Ruth Bondy
Language Editors: Art Braunstein and David Silberklang
Graphic Design: Nomi Morag
Managing Editor: Fern Seckbach

Yad Vashem wishes to thank Rabbi Walter Rothschild, Berlin,
Germany, for his initiative

© 2010 All rights reserved to Yad Vashem
P.O.B. 3477 Jerusalem 91034
publications.marketing@yadvashem.org.il

This book may not be reproduced, in whole or part,
in any form, without written permission from the publisher

Responsibility for the opinions expressed
in this publication is solely that of the author

ISBN 978-965-308-346-2
Produced by Kavim Printing Group

Contents

Foreword **6**
Helga Weissová-Hošková

And God Saw That It Was Bad **11**
Otto Weiss

About the Author **72**

Afterword: The Terezín Ghetto — A Matter of Perspective **73**
Ruth Bondy

Foreword

This little book was not originally intended for publication. It does not assess the importance of events, nor their causes. At the time and place that it was written, it had its raison d'être. It is a personal account of one man's feelings of pain and disillusionment marked by the conflict of faith with doubt, of hope with anxiety. It is an ironic comment on life in the Terezín ghetto (Theresienstadt) and the relationships among individuals, which inevitably prevailed among those whom the Nazis forced to live together in large numbers, day by day, halfway between life and death. It is a simple tale, but it is endowed with profoundly heartfelt sincerity. The pretense at humor hides much bitterness and sadness. It reveals the refined bestiality of the lying Nazi propaganda, used so effectively to hoodwink world opinion—as when a delegation of the International Committee of the Red Cross visited Terezín and accepted at face value what they were allowed to see: the Jews living "voluntarily" in a city of their own, run by their own "independent" council. At first, even the dear Lord believed it, too, in His simplicity and goodness of heart. Then, He came down to Earth and entered Terezín incognito to see for Himself. He came and He saw that it was bad.

The manuscript of the book came into being in 1943, when we did not know yet that the transports leaving for the East ended in the gas chambers, and that ultimately the men of the Ghetto-Wache (Ghetto Guards) and the so-called independent council would end up there as well.

We worked on the book during those rare moments when my father could come to see us in the evening (we did not live together in the ghetto). He was forty-five, and I was thirteen. He always brought one page with him; we talked about it, and before our next meeting I drew an illustration in the space on the page that he had left blank for me. It was our guarded secret, and when it was finished we gave it to my mother for her thirty-seventh birthday. Soon afterwards the Nazis began to liquidate the ghetto, and in October 1944 my father was among those included in a transport. He made no attempt to evade his fate, saying, "If I don't go, somebody else will have to go instead."

It was supposed to be an all-male transport dispatched to work, and father left with the faint hope that the Germans would keep their promise that the men's families would not also be sent away. That promise was not kept, and three days later mother and I were included in a transport. We were hoping to be sent to the same destination as Father. We arrived in Auschwitz. We never saw Father again.

All that remains of him is this slim book and a collection of poems, *How the Stars Were Hurting* (in Czech), which I treasure as a memory of him. Thanks to Father's encouragement, I drew over a hundred illustrations of life in Terezín. Soon after we arrived in Terezín, in December 1941, I sent him a childish drawing. His reaction was, "Draw what you see." And so I did.

Helga Weissová-Hošková

And God Saw That It Was Bad

It was a calm, pleasant January evening, full of peace and serenity, and in Heaven they were getting ready to light the stars. God was seated comfortably on His majestic throne; His bent head resting in His hands. He had just listened to the reports from His heavenly elders, still standing in a semi-circle before him and waiting in vain for their orders. With a sad face God sat motionless, gazing fixedly into space and deep in thought. What was He thinking about?

There had been nothing remarkable in the news; indeed, the elders' reports were more boring than usual. On Earth, the war had been going on for three-and-a-half years now—a terrible war, for sure, but one that was inevitable. It was not even in God's power to prevent it. Mankind no longer believed in Him; they bowed down to other gods, and it served them right! His conscience was clear; there was nothing He could do about it. Of course the innocent had to suffer along with the guilty. That was always the way of the world. He decided to give up ruling the world for a while and just watch what a mess they'd make of it without Him. He had taken care of His faithful, His Chosen People, and almost to the last He had led them from the great cities and the towns

and the tiny villages to deliver them from evil and the hatred that had run wild over half the globe. He had gathered them all together in a few large centers, crowded together so that they would not feel lost and lonely in the world gone mad. He had led them eastward and gathered them in a small town in the heart of Europe, where they could wait in peace for things to settle down; where they could work hard and serve Him.

Among those leading a God-fearing life in Terezín was one of His most faithful servants, an insignificant simple old man from Dolní Kralovice, Vítězslav Taussig. His innermost prayers rose to Heaven day after day and reached the ears of God. Vítězslav Taussig never prayed for anything for himself; he simply praised and thanked God for all His mercies. And yet, one day, his weak and broken voice betrayed what he had never actually put into words: that he was hungry. And so God sent him a parcel—but what happened? Vítězslav Taussig never even said "Thank you," which must mean that he never received the parcel. The loss of the parcel would be a shame; it contained poppy-seed buns, vanilla cookies made with butter, chocolate biscuits, apples, lemons, oranges, onions and garlic, and a whole goose liver in fat. How could such a parcel get lost? Was it conceivable that a Jew would greedily grab something that did not belong to him; something he knew belonged to one of his Jewish brethren?

And so God decided to go in person and find His devoted servant Vítězslav Taussig and help him, since help from Heaven had failed. With a slight wave of His hand He indicated to his advisers that He wished to be left alone. As his attendants retreated with low bows, He rose, packed some bare necessities into a small suitcase, sewed a yellow star onto his coat, and descended from Heaven. No one noticed His departure as He made for Terezín.

The moon had not yet risen and a heavy twilight covered the weary, resting earth, as the Lord set down foot at the Bohušovice railway station.[1]

A young man with a pan-shaped cap trimmed with a yellow ribbon and with a linen belt around his waist[2] gazed for a while in amazement at the old man with a white beard, a modest suitcase in hand. Having recovered somewhat, he gasped: "Man, where on earth have you come from?" The old man did not reply; he only smiled good-naturedly at the operetta figure, who in turn seemed to think he'd come across a loony, because he asked, "How many of you are there?"

"Just me."

---

1 From Terezín's beginnings in November 1941 until summer 1943, all transports of Jews arrived at the train station in the town of Bohušovice, and from there the deportees walked three kilometers to the walled town, laden with their luggage. An extension of the rail line into the ghetto was completed in July 1943.
2 This was the deliberately ridiculous uniform assigned to the Jewish police.

"An Einzelreisender?[3] Where've you come from?"

"From Himmelblau."[4]

"Name?"

God answered on the spur of the moment: "Aaron Gottesmann."

"Mr. Gottesmann," the young man pondered, now somewhat calmer, "you'll have to wait here until someone comes from the Transportleitung[5] to take you into the ghetto."

Aaron Gottesmann sat on a pile of wood and waited patiently. After a while, the young man turned to him and asked, as though they were old friends, "Mr. Gottesmann, what's new in the world out there? Is it true what they say about Spain? And all things considered, do you think it will really end this year?"

Aaron Gottesmann was sorry for the young fellow, gave him a pitying look and said compassionately: "My dear friend, stop worrying about such things. Leave it to God. Have faith in Him, and He will not desert you."

"My dear man, we could wait here forever and ever. In short, you don't know any more than anyone else who has arrived here. Just you wait, in a month or two you'll sing a different song."

Having said this, he disappeared into the darkness, leaving the rather shocked old man to contemplate sadly that the first person he had met here was such a disbeliever.

---

3   A single traveler; in Czech adaptation, ajnclik. Deportees from the "Protectorate of Bohemia and Moravia" usually arrived in transports of 1,000, whereas transports from Germany and Vienna usually brought several hundred people. Individuals arrived only in exceptional cases.
4   German for sky blue, or Blue Heaven.
5   Transport Administration.

It was not long before a voice could be heard approaching from the direction in which the godless young man had disappeared. "OK, where on earth is that zícha?"[6]

The voice belonged to a young man in his early twenties, but whose bearing suggested the disdain and arrogance of a brigadier general, to say the least. He was one of the brave knights of the Order of AK,[7] whom the ghetto had to thank for its foundation. There were, of course, some who envied them; someone had to be among the first, and they happened to be among them. The knight stood before Aaron Gottesmann, hands in his pockets, and shaking his head he asked: "Is that all your baggage?"

Aaron Gottesmann looked shamefacedly at his impoverished suitcase and nodded. "God help you," the brigadier general chortled. "Well, pick it up and off we go."

The brigadier general suddenly shrank to a simple conscript when he stood to attention before the Czech police sergeant[8] coming to fetch his ajnclik, followed by his ghetto policeman, whom Aaron Gottesmann already knew. The procession set out on a long, dark icy road: Aaron Gottesmann in the lead, followed by the sergeant, the ghetto guard and the AK knight of the Transportleitung bringing up the rear.

---

6   Sieche is a German word for a chronically ill person. In the ghetto dialect, *zícha* was a person near death.
7   AK, short for Aufbaukommando (construction detail), were the men of the first two transports, who had been put to work to set up the ghetto and thus assumed a privileged status.
8   In addition to SS men, there were also Czech police in the ghetto. Some of them helped inmates, while others remained indifferent, but they did not persecute them.

Soon the three of them got into an animated conversation, at times they laughed raucously. It did not seem as if these people were suffering too much hardship. They were particularly amused at the first mention of the word šlojs.⁹ Aaron Gottesmann had never heard the word before, and it took him a long time to fully understand it.

It seemed to be a mysterious word of many meanings; a noun used as a verb, the verb had alternately active and passive meanings. There was something exceedingly funny about it, but at the same time it had horrifying undertones.

"Where'll we šlojs him?" the ghetto policeman asked. There could be no mistake about it—"him" was Aaron Gottesmann. Was this an initiation ceremony into some secret society?

9   Šlojs, or Schleuse in German, is a sluice. Conjugated and declined in an ironic Czech version, it referred to the reception area where the new arrivals were checked, and where the SS confiscated part of their belongings. Some were confiscated for the needs of the ghetto, and the workers at the site stole some for themselves. In its various forms and conjugations, the word referred to the place where this took place, the fact of being searched, and the active "claiming" of belongings by those in charge. The term *šlojs* became a synonym for stealing from the collective goods. Those being deported to the East were also gathered in a *šlojska* before they were sent off.

"In Magdeburg, I suppose,"[10] the sergeant answered, "but just look at him. He hasn't got anything. That sort of šlojs I can do without. Now next week, when we šlojs Prague, that'll be quite different."

"They say there'll be twelve hundred," the AK knight spoke up. "Good grief folks, that will make me sick again. Last time I couldn't eat anything for a whole week."

"My old lady's birthday is in two weeks," the ghetto policeman said. "I'll have to šlojs a decent pair of shoes for her; the old ones are completely worn out. I hope I'll be on duty at the šlojs."

"I'm not worried about you," the sergeant teased, "you'll always wangle some black marketeering." He dipped into his pocket and pulled out a cigarette case. "Here you are, lads." He halved one cigarette for the two and lit a second one for himself. "Look out, though, or there'll be trouble."[11]

The journey went quickly, and less than an hour had passed when they entered the gate of the Magdeburg barracks. The clerk who registered Aaron Gottesmann could not understand how anyone could exist on earth without an identity card, but finally he accepted a confused story about the special circumstances of his trek.

So far everything had gone smoothly and without any great difficulties. But there must have been something mysterious about the ceremony of

---

10 Magdeburg and other names of German towns designated the barracks in the ghetto. The names had been designated by the German army, which had been stationed there from the March 1939 occupation until they were transferred for the creation of the ghetto. In the ghetto slang, the word "barrack" was dropped, and only the city names remained.

11 Jews were forbidden to buy or smoke cigarettes even before the deportations to the ghetto. Anyone caught smoking in the ghetto could be severely punished by the SS.

šlojsing, for, although Aaron Gottesmann was sure he hadn't let his case out of his sight for a moment, he discovered later that his bath soap, along with his toothbrush, toothpaste, a packet of chocolate and a bag of biscuits, which he had brought for Vitězslav Taussig, were missing.

At last, he was an acknowledged ghetto inmate, his name forever linked with transport number EZ 205 and a tiny space allotted to him in Q 715.[12] The Hausältester[13] declared that he had no room for him, but the Transportleitung clerk insisted that this was where his charge was going to live, and so Aaron Gottesmann had to be content with what was not exactly the most comfortable makeshift bed. Yet he slept well, perhaps because of his unaccustomed fatigue. When he woke the next morning, his roommates were coming in with mugs of black coffee. It had no aroma and gave off no steam, but he would have liked a drink. He realized at that moment that he had not thought to bring a mug or plate with him. His neighbor, a shriveled ugly old man with a large goiter, instinctively seemed to know his trouble; he nudged him and without a word gave him the dregs of his coffee.

"You'll have to find some kind of utensil; you can't go on like this," he said in a matter-of-fact voice.

"But how?" Aaron Gottesmann asked.

"That's very difficult; but get hold of a couple of cigarettes, and I'll manage something for you by this evening."

---

12 The ghetto streets had letter designations rather than names — L (length) and Q (width, or cross streets). Buildings were designated by letter and number. Street names were later assigned only as part of the preparations for the visit of the International Committee of the Red Cross.

13 Elder of the house, who was house boss.

Aaron Gottesmann had not the slightest intention of revealing his incognito, but he did not like the feeling that everybody regarded him with disdain and acted harshly. He was amazed, too, that he felt so powerless, unable even to get hold of a mug for drinking. Indeed, he began to doubt his own divine nature. Was it because he had come down to Earth and had lost his divine powers, that they were valid only in Heaven? That was a debatable matter. He had always relied on his Council of Elders in everything; they told him where His help was needed, and He had always assumed His orders would be carried out. And here he was discovering things he had never dreamed of. If he did not put matters right, his throne would be endangered. First of all,

however, he would investigate everything himself; and the first thing he'd do when he got back to Heaven would be to sack the Council of Elders and appoint a new Cabinet.

He tidied his makeshift bed and set out to find Vitězslav Taussig. They sent him to the central registration card index which was in Magdeburg. He took his place in the endless queue that did not move one inch. The only hope of progress seemed to be when one of those waiting got too exhausted, and left. When he got as far as the clerk sitting under the letter T, he asked after Vitězslav Taussig.

"Transport number?"

"I'm afraid I don't know." The clerk's expression was desperate. "For God's sake, man, do you have any idea how much work that means?"

"Still, if you wouldn't mind ..."

An angry look and the clerk started going through his cards. It turned out that not counting those Taussigs who had left for the East, there were 182 in Terezín and fourteen of them had the given name Vítězslav.

Aaron Gottesmann spent the whole morning trying to track down his Vítězslav Taussig, but none of those he found came from Dolní Kralovice. There were five more left, but he decided to leave them for the afternoon. Now it was time to eat, because he was really feeling hungry.

There was a mug and a bowl on his bed. His neighbor had been as good as his word. But where was he going to get hold of those two cigarettes? He took his bowl and joined the queue, as endless as the one in the office—but this time nobody thought of giving up his place. The man ahead of him, affecting innocence, asked an elegant white-haired lady in a fashionable hat, who must have come from the Altreich: "Do you happen to know what kind of soup is on the menu today, madam?"[14] The lady looked the man who had posed the question up and down and spluttered something about cheek and her noble birth. It took several days before Aaron Gottesmann fully understood this episode. That day, however, he ate his soup, which for some unknown reason was called Linsensuppe.[15] He was just finishing his potatoes dipped in gravy when his neighbor entered, smiling kindly. He shrugged off the overwhelming expression of gratitude for the bowl and mug saying, "Don't mention it.

---

14 Elderly Jews from Germany were told that they were being sent to a senior citizens' home. They dressed accordingly and brought nothing useful with them. It took time before they realized their true situation.

15 Lentil soup. In fact, this gray, bitter liquid was made of lentil peels.

And you needn't go looking for cigarettes, it didn't cost me anything. Someone died last night in the next room; he got Terezínka[16] and I thought of you."

Aaron Gottesmann fell on his makeshift bed and tried to get some rest.

"Tired, eh?"

"Just a bit. I spent all morning running around looking for someone. I'll try again this afternoon, maybe I'll find him."

"May I ask who it is you're looking for?"

"He's called Vítězslav Taussig."

"Well I never, and seeing I asked politely, you can give me a straight answer, can't you? You don't have to get upset straight away."

"Upset? What makes you think that? All I said was, I'm looking for Vítězslav Taussig of Dolní Kralovice."

"And why should you spend time looking for him when he is right here next to you? Vítězslav Taussig—that's me."

Aaron Gottesmann lifted his head and sat up on his makeshift bed. Chance, fate, or the hand of God, as people say? It is His Supreme Will that people and the world should exist in a firm and distinct order relative to each other. His Will is Law, which so orders events that they follow His Will. God Himself could not attend to such small details, of course, He had no time for that, but things would work out as they should. It might be that the Raumwirtschaft[17] frequently told the Transportleitung that there were free places where there were none, but

---

16 Slang for Enteritis, characteristic of conditions in Terezín, caused by the poor food conditions. For the elderly and ill it was often a death sentence.

17 The word used for the Housing Administration and for craft work spaces.

in such cases the mistake had a profound meaning incomprehensible to ordinary humans. Such as when enteritis finished off one poor creature, whose bed would straightaway be taken by someone from Gottesmann's room, who was waiting for the opportunity to move into the room where his brother-in-law was, and that someone's bed would be taken over by Aaron Gottesmann, who in addition would inherit the dead man's mug, something essential to ghetto life but unobtainable in the Materialverwaltung,[18] where they had no mugs.

"So what's on your mind? For Heaven's sake tell me what you're doing here."

"I came to Terezín because of you," Aaron Gottesmann said without thinking.

"What's that supposed to mean, because of me?"

And now, how could he get out of that quandary? He could not tell the truth, because that would land him in the lunatic asylum, or else Vítězslav Taussig would suffer a stroke. And so God lied: "Well, last week I was waiting in the queue at the Ostrovní Street Post Office, in Prague,[19] and the woman ahead of me was handing in a parcel addressed to you. I said to myself, 'let's hope the poor fellow gets it!' Someone overheard me, informed on me, and here I am, an Einzelreisender."

"I can't say how sorry I am, but you must be more careful next time. What did the lady look like?"

"I don't really know, but I think she was of slight build."

---

18 Supplies Administration.
19 This was the only post office that the Jews in Prague were permitted to use and from which they could send packages to loved ones in Terezín.

"That would have been my niece, she's arisch versippt[20] and so she hasn't had to come here.

"That's right, I remember now, she said it was a parcel for her uncle from Dolní Kralovice. Did you get it?"

"You want to know whether I got it? You'd like to have a taste of the goodies, would you? Too bad, though I would have been only too happy to share it with you."

"God forbid! What do you think of me? I just wanted to find out if it is true that everything gets lost here."

"What do you mean 'gets lost'? That Linsensuppe we had today, or the infested bed-linen of the Siechen, that's about all you can leave lying around here."

"What you say is sad indeed."

"Unfortunately, there are even sadder things." Vitězslav Taussig heaved a deep sigh.

"May I ask what can be sadder?"

"You'll find out soon enough—maybe this very evening."

And indeed, the town had been experiencing mounting distress and unusual tension for several days. Those who had been in Terezín for some time recognized this mood. Whoever experienced it would not forget it until his dying day.

20 A Nazi term meaning having Aryan family.

"Is it true that the summons for Poland will be distributed today?" This question hung in the air, reflected in everyone's anxious expression. Whether spoken aloud or not, it concealed the terror of people who thought they had come safely through all their trials, only to be confronted with a new, unknown threat, perhaps worse than all that had gone before.

Simple people, with no highly developed intellect, had a heightened sense for such things. They were usually earlier and better informed than those near to where the preparations for a transport were being made. Perhaps it is because they were most threatened, and they needed to be ready to protect themselves.

Vitězslav Taussig was one of those who had every right to feel in great personal danger. In that newly formed society of Terezín he was on one of the lowest rungs of the social ladder. He was one of the Wasserdienst, the service for guarding the consumption of water. He did his job conscientiously and was glad to serve, he was not begrudging nor did he behave officiously, and he never spoke harshly. He had plenty of opportunity to observe human weakness; he smiled, feeling sorry for the poor old people; he liked them and they liked him. He was well liked, but what was that compared to having a relative in the Ältestenrat,[21] or at least in the stab,[22] and he did not have anybody. There was no question of pleading that his family ought not to be broken up, for his family

---

21 Council of Elders. This was the Jewish self-administration, appointed by the SS and headed by Jacob Edelstein. The Nazis did not believe that the Jews were worthy of titles such as "director," and preferred the archaic term "elder."

22 The headquarters. This was a group of twenty-two men and women volunteers who were closely associated with Edelstein.

had been broken up long before, and in a manner which served as no argument in the current situation as far as officialdom was concerned. He had been widowed eight years earlier, his daughter married and left for Buenos Aires in 1938; his son did not appear either in the first or in the second contingent of the AK, because he had simply gone off to London.

If at least he had gone to Palestine; that was an argument that some listened to here. What else was there? Sickness? A weak heart, arteriosclerosis and rheumatism were not enough to be excused from transport. The last time he had been lucky; a common flu, but the thermometer showed exactly 39.5°C at the right moment during the doctor's examination. What if he were to turn to the only influential man he knew in Terezín, a fellow student and friend of his son's, Dr. Spiegel. He had met him once—you must excuse the place, but it was in the latrines. Dr. Spiegel was delighted to hear that Jirka was doing well, and of his own accord said, "Mr. Taussig, you know what friends Jirka and I were; if ever you need something, you know where to find me."

When he told Aaron Gottesmann about this meeting, he got a comforting reply. "You see, now, God has not deserted you. It was His doing that you met Dr. Spiegel, and now he'll be of use to you."

"Don't laugh, Mr. Gottesmann, but the fact that we met was not God's work. It was diarrhea that sent Dr. Spiegel into our building; he was just passing by when he had to go. I'd like to bet that God doesn't even know there's a Dr. Spiegel alive in the world. And even if He did know—not even God can sway the selection committee. Anyway, I've

long since come to the conclusion that God doesn't exist. How could He possibly suffer in silence what's going on nowadays?"

There was so much disillusion and bitterness in Taussig's voice that Aaron Gottesmann could not bring himself to be angry. He put his arm around the other's shoulders and tried to soothe him: "Now, now, just calm down and don't let me hear talk like that again. Anyway, it's time we were going, isn't it?"

It was getting dark, which was nothing to look forward to on these short days in January. The Almighty was very surprised to hear that the people of Terezín, in addition to all the other burdens they had to bear, were visited by yet another Egyptian plague: Lichtsperre!²³ Every third day the use of electric light, paraffin lamps, candles and not to mention flashlights, was forbidden in one barrack or another; life went on in complete darkness. What was worse, one never knew whether the electric light would work when it was allowed and supposed to, or whether there would be another emergency blackout, which usually happened on days of exceptional confusion, like that very day.

"Well, here we are again," the Zimmerältester [room elder] said as he came in. There was nothing unusual about his voice; he might have been announcing the next day's bread ration. Everybody in the room knew what it was about, of course; they grew pale, silent, and waited tensely. The door opened, and in came the Hausältester, holding slips of paper in his hand. He heaved a sigh, shrugged his shoulders, and read out a few names in a low voice. One of them was Taussig's; another was Gottesmann's. They looked at each other with mutual empathy, put on their coats, and went out.

The Magdeburg barracks were a madhouse that evening—not that it was far from being such on any other day. People filled the corridors, running senselessly back and forth, asking where this or that office was, but usually asking for one specific place, asking where so-and-so had his office, one of the few who could settle the fate of tens of thousands. Hundreds and hundreds of people pressed up against a few doors, protected like a fortress by shouting and yelling ghetto guards and

---

23 This was the ban on turning on lights that was sometimes imposed by the SS as collective punishment and was at times applied because of the overtaxing of the town's electric capacity, which had originally been designed to support 7,000 inhabitants, not 50,000 or more.

OD men.[24] These crowds, subdued, concentrated on a single purpose: their fight for their own lives, and for those dearest to them, and each encouraged the other. Those who tried to defend the fortress could not

24 OD was the Ordnungsdienst, or Order Service, whose job was to maintain order in food lines and other assembly points.

see why the crowd could not be silenced, why the women who were hysterically weeping and screaming wouldn't just go home, since there was nothing they could alter, anyway. It's easy for them to talk! These people had not been in Terezín long, but they had immediately known how to manage things as if by instinct, and they were all eager to take on duties of the lowest social level, fully aware of how they would be despised. What did it matter? For the moment they had been saved, they and their families, and they did not have to fear for the morrow like those listed for transport. Naturally, there was confusion and unrest inside the office, where tired, dispassionate clerks had to listen to hundreds of personal dramas, heartbreaking and incomprehensibly involved. What could they do but write a sentence or two on the cards that they piled up because the commission would begin to assess all these cases after midnight. They could not say "yes" or "no"; they could give little hope, and the only practical advice they gave was: pack your things anyway!

Our two friends waited two hours in the queue before they had completed all the formalities, which seemed in vain because only one thing seemed clear: they did not want to be sent to Poland.

Dr. Spiegel was not in his office because his whereabouts were kept secret. By chance the two men caught a whispered conversation behind them; otherwise it would not have occurred to them that the lawyer would be having supper at home. Vitězslav Taussig knocked on the door several times before a key rattled in the lock and only after he said his name did the door really open.

He had seen nothing but poor, filthy residencies all the time he had been in Terezín, and never really believed the rumors told by evil-minded people about the way the people at the top lived in the lap of luxury. Admittedly, people are evil; it was indeed true that those in the soft jobs knew how to look after themselves. This young couple had two whole rooms to themselves, light and airy, tastefully furnished with little tables, cushions, carpets, a white cloth on the table and  what a dinner! Not the half ounce of margarine and the ersatz coffee that was the ration for that day, but delicatessen, recalling a time long past, served on glassware and china. When he saw it with his own eyes, Vitězslav Taussig clenched his fist in anger, crumpling the slip of paper he still held. He would have turned round and left, but Dr. Spiegel was already introducing him to his wife. "This is Jirka Taussig's father, Veruška. Remember my telling you I used to share rooms with him in Prague. What a pity you didn't come sooner, Mr. Taussig, the place is a madhouse today."

"I wouldn't have come today either, but it's just because Mr. Gottesmann here and I are in trouble now that I have taken the liberty. Would it be possible to help us? Understandably, I really don't want to go to Poland."

"Do sit down, gentlemen. Veruška, please pour us a cup of tea? The situation's really bad just now. I'll do what I can, of course, but by morning we've got to have a list of one thousand names ready for the transport."

Aaron Gottesmann had never imagined he would ever find himself helplessly unable to do anything for just one man, as he stood before a member of the appeals commission. All he could think of was: "Perhaps you'll be able to help him, Mr. Taussig's had a hard life and he deserves to be let off."

"I'll see, gentlemen, as I said. Let me have your transport numbers. I'm afraid you'll have to go through the šlojs, though, to avoid any unpleasantness. Well, let's hope we can pull it off, and then you must come and celebrate with us. Now you must excuse me, I've got that commission meeting."

As they passed along the dark corridors still full of people, they heard chatter and laughter at the far end. There was a new revue that evening in the hall. "What are all these people fussing about?" a woman asked her companion, and he calmed her gently as they went in: "It's nothing, just another transport going East."

It was after eleven when they got back to their room, and as they feared, there was no electricity.

One feeble candle flickered in the corner, where eleven of the twenty-two inmates were trying to pack the few miserable possessions they had left. There was not enough light to see what they were doing, they had to tell by touch whether what they'd got hold of was a shirt or a towel or underpants. The appeals commission would start work at midnight, and at eight in the morning they'd all go through the šlojs. By that time, the appeal would have to come through, or it would be too late. What trivial things occupied their minds as they prepared to journey into the unknown: Is it worthwhile taking these old shoes? What if I took my wooden shelf and made it into a handcart on runners, for my bags? But what will I do for a shelf, if I stay here after all? There were only a few hours left to decide all these problems, more important than they seemed at first sight; only a few hours in which to get hold of what they needed, to get clean underwear from the laundry,[25] or mend worn soles, to say farewell to family and friends—and these were sick men, aging and exhausted, feeling their way round in the dark.

Vitězslav Taussig behaved with admirable dignity and seemed quite calm, but at one moment even he burst out: "The dirty scoundrels! We're not even worth a bit of candle. We can go and croak in Poland for them, that's fine, so long as they can live like lords, but would they make it easier for us? That they would not do. They're all scoundrels!"

Aaron Gottesmann had no need to hurry; morning would be time enough for the little he had with him. He lay on his bed and dozed a while, wondering at the mess he'd got himself into and how he could get out of it. Not only did he want to help these poor creatures, he also wanted to prove to himself that all things living and inanimate were subject to His will. And so Aaron Gottesmann said: "Let there be light!"—but darkness prevailed.

---

25 Ghetto residents were permitted to have their underwear laundered in the central laundry once every few weeks. This was done according to a list, and the laundry had to be submitted in a package bearing the owner's transport number. The laundry was returned clean in a few days.

Towards morning three of the men on that day's list were eliminated from the transport. The others had to go to the šlojs, by now with only a glimmer of hope. The šlojs! What a pity that Dante did not live to see Terezín—he would not have had to draw on his fantasy for effect. Only the most prejudiced would deny that much had been done in Terezín for medical care and hygiene, even for social needs. Yet it must be laid at the door of those responsible for their fellows that they took little thought to make life easier for those whose departure for the east, from time to time, helped those left behind to enjoy a somewhat more human life for a while.

The thousands who left through the gate of the Ústí[26] barracks were no longer regarded as human beings. All the lowest instincts of those monsters in their belts and buttons were unleashed and allowed to run wild. Cruelty, outrage, greed and indifference to the sufferings of others, lack of respect for those older and weaker than oneself, were given free rein, and orgies of cruelty ensued. The Jewish authorities knew well enough what was going on, but they did nothing to prevent it. On the contrary, they had or took unheard-of privileges, allowing them to live with their families and enjoy all the luxury of an upper class.

A day spent in the šlojs seemed three times as long as any other—there was no end to the uncertainty and the waiting. A name would be called from time to time, a transport number telling one happy man that he had not waited in vain. Another slip of paper, but how much more cheerful, more welcome! Ausgeschieden! [Exempt!] Joy for one man

---

26 The Germans used the German town name, Aussig, for these barracks, while the Czech Jews used the Czech name.

meant even less hope for the others. All at once there was an important announcement, judging from the reactions of those listening. What did they say? All those over sixty were to be left behind. Vitězslav Taussig was just fifty-nine.

"This is where we say goodbye, Mr. Gottesmann."

"Time enough, let's wait and see whether your appeal's been heard."

"May I preserve my health, and I'm on my way. I didn't believe it from the first moment. Why did I bother going to that Dr. Spiegel?"

He was silent for a long time, his lips pursed. Then he shrugged. "Can't be helped; to hell with it!"

A moment later, not looking up from the ground, he said: "Mr. Gottesmann, look here, I've got more stuff with me than I need, and they won't let me take it with me, anyway. You've got so little and you're staying on here. Be so good as to take one of my suitcases."

"What an idea! Instead of being of some use to you, I'm going to be indebted to you?"

"For God's sake, don't start arguing. Take care of it for me, if you like, and you'll give it back to me after the war. OK?" He said it with such a good-natured laugh, the way only the really good-hearted know how to laugh.

Vitězslav Taussig lost that depressive feeling of self-pitying hopelessness common to all outcasts. Instead he sensed a new calm, dignity, and even a pleasant pain of one who was rejecting a nasty world that had been so cruel to him.

As he stumbled along the road to the station, muddy but prudently made free of onlookers, he tried to look neither to the right nor to the left, not even at the windows of the "elect" of the ghetto.

He did not cease to believe in God, although he had complained about Him more than once to his friend Aaron Gottesmann. He forgave Him His lack of interest in one insignificant Jew, since He was concerned with much more important things. In the end, he was convinced that if God knew about him and his miserable life, He would befriend him and not let him be taken away to die in Poland.

There was nobody he could say goodbye to, not even the grave old man who had become his friend, but who was fast asleep at the moment when his number was called.

The train had not yet left the Bohušovice station when the little town recovered, as if waking from a narcotic sleep. It breathed in deep relief

at the thought that the danger had passed, although no one could say for how long. It was a time when one lived from day to day, and nobody lived otherwise. There was something akin to cannibalism in the way people calmly accepted that another thousand of them had left, and that they had family and friends among them.

Friends meeting in front of the Dresden barracks greeted each other:

"Thank God you've got out of it this time, my congratulations, there's a God above us after all, there's justice in this world."

Aaron Gottesmann passed by at that moment and thought to himself: the thousand who have just left may not agree with you.

From the šlojs, he went back to his place in Q 715, but there seemed to be no happy feeling that he and three other old men had come back. That poor man Vitězslav Taussig had made him his universal heir, but when he returned to the building, he found that the "dead" man's effects had been appropriated by others. One Max Israel Cohen was comfortably stretched out on Taussig's bed by the window; he had come from Berlin, and pretended to be asleep. By a magnificent effort at adaptation, Taussig's shelf had become a two-shelf edifice, the lower shelf serving as a bedside table for one Herzfeld of Brno, who had spread a white cloth over it, not so much for hygienic reasons as to stress ownership. Aaron Gottesmann could only capitulate to such faits accomplis, since Taussig's will had been given only orally. And so he stayed on the darkest bed in the worst corner. There he laid out Taussig's case, noticing meanwhile that Herzfeld was looking at him strangely. If only he didn't feel so tired and aching after the šlojs, he wouldn't have come back here at all, but he needed a wash and a rest, at least for a day or two. It took more effort to climb into the upper bunk than to rise to the upper Heavens. He had just time to make his bunk comfortable when sleep came. But not for long. A rasping voice woke him: "Get moving, you're on Klodienst [latrine duty][27] from one to two." He could not fall asleep again in case he overslept, and anyway he was curious about the job ahead. And the man opposite, a Mr. Pentlička from

---

27 This was the ghetto's shortened colloquial version of the German word Klosettdienst.

Prague, was groaning all the time: "Ach Gott, ach Gott!" It surprised him that Pentlička used the God-forsaken German language when he actually wanted to call on Him, but he whispered nevertheless: "Did you want something?"

"Hey, mind your own business, will you, I've got nothing to do with you."

"I thought you called my name," Aaron Gottesmann said thoughtlessly.

"Your name? You must be crazy!"

Why was everybody so touchy and cantankerous!

The clock in the tower[28] struck a quarter to one, and Aaron Gottesmann got ready for duty at the latrines.

Klodienst! This low and apparently insignificant function was very differently viewed by different people. Some thought it was meant to provide statistics about who used the latrines and when, men or women, at what times, for what bodily function, what effect various liquids taken at supper had, and so on. Others thought it was a social occasion, and described all that happened in technical detail. Others took their duty to

---

28 Like other Czech towns, Terezín had a church with a clock tower. It had been locked following the exit of the Czech population, but the clock continued to mark time.

mean they could trace those using the latrines by what they left behind, and punish them. The nature of the function, however, induced most people to strike up a close acquaintance with those waiting their turn. It suited them since it lessened the boredom of waiting. Sometimes the tales told were short; at other times they were long, long stories.

Aaron Gottesmann took up his position with dignity in the cold, grim and badly lit corridor and prepared to wait.

Soon sleepy figures appeared, dressed in rags, and the shuffle of slippers never ceased. All the inmates of his room turned up: the arrogant Max Israel Cohen, the cunning Herzfeld, and even Pentlička. The latter had to wait a long time, and at first embarrassed and grumbling, gradually softened enough to say: "I'm sorry I snapped at you; we've all had troubles enough, and after a few days like I've just had one's ready to commit murder."

"Tell me your troubles, there's a cure for all things."

"What's happened to me has happened to thousands more, it's nothing out of the ordinary in these days of unheard-of cruelty. I buried my wife not a week ago. She cut a finger while she was slicing bread, she got blood poisoning and two days later she was dead. The day of the funeral[29] my only daughter had surgery on her middle ear, and we still don't know the result. Can you imagine what she felt like when they took her away? Two children sick with typhus, and she hadn't seen her husband for two years;

---

29 There were no real funerals in Terezín. A deceased's relatives were permitted to accompany the body as far as the storage point for bodies within the town walls. A horse-drawn wagon would take many bodies out in simple wood coffins to the crematorium outside the ghetto, where the bodies were incinerated.

they told her he had died in the Small Fortress.[30] I've got only one sister. She's got tuberculosis and she lost her husband a month ago. They put her on the transport list and nothing I could do got her off. She went, and my nephew who came with the L-transport[31] and worked himself to the bone went voluntarily in a transport with his wife and children. Don't you think that's enough for one man? Believe me, I've never said a blasphemous word, but I'd like to hear someone tell me this is how things should be. I've never done any harm, I believed in God all my life, and He's just let me down. You've nothing to say to that, eh? Whatever you say would only be empty words. But I went at you as though it was your fault, and you're just as downtrodden as I am, aren't you?"

Aaron Gottesman kept silent, because he could find no words to answer such a flow of reproaches, and he was glad somebody came to

30   The Small Fortress was the feared Terezín Gestapo prison whence few came out alive. The garrison town Terezín was sometimes called the Large Fortress.
31   Transports into and out of the ghetto were denoted by letters in alphabetical order. The L-transport arrived on December 5, 1941, shortly after the ghetto was created. Otto Weiss and his wife and daughter also arrived in the ghetto at that time.

take his place before Pentlička came back from the latrine and started talking again.

"Note: Take a look at the card index, Rudolf Pentlička, Prague-Smíchov," Aaron Gottesmann wrote on a piece of toilet paper.[32] He was not sorry he had come down to Earth, not at all. He was angry with his advisers who had kept the true state of affairs from him. They had never so much as mentioned the plague of fleas that gave these hard-tried people no rest even at night, as he had found out for himself. This was a grave misdemeanor, and his subordinates would be properly punished.

What did His people think of Him? He determined to put things right as soon as he returned to Heaven, and to punish those responsible. They'd have the fright of their lives! He had hardly gotten dressed next morning when a grim-faced man asked his name:

"Are you Aaron Gottesmann?"

He nodded silently.

"How did you get hold of this case?"

"My friend Vítězslav Taussig gave it me ..."

"Shut your mouth, you liar! You stole it," the Kripouš[33] shouted, having shown his card, proving himself to be one of Löwenzahn's[34] universally dreaded criminal police.

---

32 Toilet paper, and any kind of paper, was a valuable commodity in the ghetto. When there was no toilet paper, people used wet rags that they rinsed after use.

33 Short for the German word Kriminalpolizei, criminal police.

34 This is a modification of the name of the second commander of the ghetto police, Dr. Karl Löwenstein, a former German officer decorated in World War I, who had also been adjutant to the German crown prince. He had been sent to Terezín from the Riga ghetto in May 1942 on SS orders and enjoyed a privileged status.

"God is my witness that what I said is the truth." Gottesmann had no other way of defending himself against such a terrible accusation.

"Then bring him here to testify. I can bring witnesses who say something very different. You're old enough to know what it means to steal a suitcase in the šlojs."

"I tell you once again that I was given this case by my friend Taussig."

"Your friend, eh? You've known him for a couple of days. Taussig gave his suitcase to Mr. Herzfeld here, and you were supposed to hand it over to him. Somebody else who came back from the šlojs came to ask whether Herzfeld had received the suitcase."

"Mr. Taussig said nothing of the sort, I swear, and I'd like to see the man you're talking about," Aaron Gottesmann felt bold enough to add.

"You'd better take care what you say. Mr. Herzfeld, did that man come here and tell you, or did he not?"

"Of course he was here," Herzfeld was almost too sure. "When was that?"

"Yesterday evening. And here I've got it written down," he said haughtily and gave the Kripouš a piece of paper.

"What've you got to say to that?" the Kripouš shouted triumphantly.

"Why didn't Mr. Herzfeld show me that paper sooner? I had no idea I was supposed to hand the suitcase over to him." He placed the fateful case at Herzfeld's feet. "Here you are."

"That means you admit to the crime? You couldn't do anything else, could you? You'll hear more about this from the Ghettogericht [ghetto court].[35] Good evening, gentlemen," and he left before Aaron Gottesmann had recovered from his astonishment.

There was embarrassed silence in the room, and nobody dared raise his eyes, let alone speak. It was a relief for all when the Zimmerältester came in from next door and said, as though catastrophe had struck: "Gentlemen, you can't keep the Tagesbefehl [order of the day][36] that long! You know we are waiting for it!"

They handed it over and he muttered something and disappeared.

The ghetto bureaucracy was complex. If you write your curriculum

---

35 Terezín had a ghetto court of the Jewish administration that adjudicated in matters of internal regulations. Violations of SS orders were dealt with severely by the SS without trial.

36 The Tagesbefehl included SS instructions and a notice from the Jewish administration and was brought to the barracks for ghetto inmates' information.

vitae here, in the hope of achieving a promotion, you don't say how old you are; you just give your birth date, thus avoiding possible reproaches if you are called to appear. If you want to have your watch mended,[37] you first find out how the most complicated administrative system in this world works. If you need to replace a worn-out shirt, you arm yourself with all the patience in the world and harbor no illusions about the quality of what you are about to receive—unless you happen to know someone in the Verteilungsstelle [distribution center],[38] or unless you happen to have half a loaf of bread left over from the last handout.

Yet there is one authority that works surprisingly fast: the Sicherheitswesen [security office].[39] That very afternoon Aaron Gottesman was handed a warrant to appear the next day.

Fully confident in the wisdom and justice of the judges of a people with such a long tradition of civilization, he went to the Magdeburg barracks at the set time. His confidence sprang from his absolute innocence and his belief that this innocence would be clearly proven. He was even surer of himself when Mr. Pentlička came up to him first thing in the morning and explained happily:

"Mr. Gottesmann, that story of the suitcase worried me all night. Now I understand it. When you appear before the judge you must stress that Herzfeld was just a bit too clever with his piece of paper."

---

37 All wristwatches were confiscated from Jews upon arrival in the ghetto and were sent to the soldiers at the front. Only physicians and some other professionals who needed watches for their work were given special dispensation to have one.

38 By special permission, prisoners could receive clothing and shoes of prisoners who died or had been deported, in place of their completely worn-out clothing.

39 This office included the ghetto police, firefighters, Kripo, and Ordnungsdienst.

"What do you mean, too clever?"

"Ježíšmarja,⁴⁰ didn't you see? He said he'd been given the paper the evening before last, but he forgot it couldn't have been written sooner than yesterday morning."

"What makes you think so?"

---

40 Czech for Jesus Mary. Czech Jews were generally so acculturated that they used the same Christian exclamations as their Czech countrymen, rather than a Jewish or non-denominational exclamation.

"You must have been born yesterday! It was written on the back of the Tagesbefehl, and that wasn't here before morning!"

"Well, I never, that didn't occur to me. Thank you for telling me, and thank you for believing I wouldn't have done such a thing."

"Of course you wouldn't, anyone can tell

that. But people are so evil-minded here; maybe it's all God's punishment on us all. The decent ones are the worse off, though, and the scoundrels get away with it. Just you tell them, they'll have to eat their words."

He accompanied Aaron Gottesmann right to the courthouse, and shook his hand heartily. This was the first time he had walked through the streets of the ghetto during the day, and he was astonished at the dilapidated, bleak facades, all alike as peas in a pod. What had once been shop-windows displayed the remnants of a half-nomadic way of life, the ruins of what had once been decent households.

Every other window had broken panes, stuck together with ugly strips of wrapping paper, or replaced with packing-cases or cardboard. Where it was possible to look in, the scene was always the same:

crowded cages, bunks of two or three tiers, right up to the windows, and only a narrow space between each. There were crowds about, and they all seemed bent on some important goal. Labor brigades with picks and shovels, young lads and girls, men and women with briefcases under their arms, old men with jugs and buckets of apparently valuable content. The road was full of carts loaded mysteriously, the most noticeable being elegant two-wheeled vehicles somewhat reminiscent of Chinese rickshaws, drawn by men in white coats, and bearing a lightly covered load of skinny human bodies. Why did they not use hearses to move the dead?[41] Perhaps because the hearses were needed to carry bread, baggage of all sorts, lice-ridden and deloused clothing and bed linen. What was that? Surely not meat? Yes, indeed it was meat, and whole carcasses. Why had Vitězslav Taussig, who was the most truthful of men, said that he'd never touched meat here? Perhaps meat was so rare that people raised their hats to it. Or were they raising them to the young man on the hurtling tractor, with a grim face, wearing no star but a fiat cap with a shining peak [an SS man]?[42] Aaron Gottesmann doffed his hat as did all those in the street, but perhaps it was not meant for the young man, since he did not reciprocate.

"Rechts gehen [right turn]," a bestrapped OD guard said at the entrance to Magdeburg. Then, "Ach, Verzeihung, entschuldigen Sie,

41   Nearly all transport in the ghetto was via rickshaws pulled by the ghetto inmates. For this purpose, wagons that had been used as hearses by *Hevrot Kadisha* (burial societies) in the Jewish communities of Bohemia and Moravia that had been liquidated, were now being used for various purposes, such as transporting bread, supplies, ill people, and luggage.
42   The more senior SS men were rarely seen in the ghetto. The junior SS men served as drivers of official vehicles and tractors (Jews were forbidden to drive vehicles of any sort). Jewish men were obligated to remove their hats before Germans.

bitte," [Oh, sorry, excuse me] and he was at the mercy of poor old men and fearful grannies, looking for the Fürsorge, Wirschaftsamt, Bezugscheinstelle[43] and other official places. It was by pure chance if you found the room-number you were looking for in Magdeburg. Numbers went up or down suddenly, or came to an end, and nobody could tell you where to go. At last he found the door he was looking for.

"We'll call you in about half an hour, just wait here." And so he waited, not for half an hour but for an hour and three quarters, before they called him in. There were three members of the court, very reputable looking men. The charge was of embezzlement, of failing to hand over a suitcase—simple, sober, calm words.

"Your honor," the accused answered in a firm voice, "there can be no question of embezzlement. Mr. Taussig did not ask me to hand over the case. He gave it to me."

"Then why did he send a message to Mr. Herzfeld?"

"He sent no message. It was not Mr. Taussig, but someone else who wrote that message."

"Now why do you say that?"

"It's quite simple. The message was written on the back of the Tagesbefehl, which Mr. Taussig could not have had in his hands, because it was brought to our room the next day after the transport had left, and it was brought in by the Zimmerältester, from next door, who came to ask for it back, later."

"Do you mean to say it was a forgery?"

---

43 Social welfare; the economics office; the office that issued vouchers for rationed goods and services.

"That's the only way I can explain it. "

"And don't you think our clerk would have noticed that?"

"If he had noticed it, I wouldn't be here now."

The judge, who had sat quietly so far, went red in the face and shouted: "Another word and you'll find yourself accused of insulting officials of the ghetto administration. Do you know what that entails? Have you got anything more to say about the case under judgment?"

"I have already said what had to be said, and I await your just decision."

After a short consultation the court issued its verdict: guilty. The accused was sentenced to three months imprisonment, with two days a month without warm food, and no right to official appointments in the ghetto.

"Gentlemen, I beg you ..."

"Don't waste our time, we can't listen to nonsense. Mr. Singer, bring in the next accused."

Sad and disillusioned, Aaron Gottesmann went home; he looked at no one, and they all turned their backs on him anyway. Only Pentlička asked him curiously how it had gone.

"I've been sentenced," the old man said in desperation, lying down and covering his head. Only recently, the whole ghetto was alive with the exciting news that traveled from transports AII to JIV[44] that a high

---

[44] Incoming transports from the Protectorate were designated by letters, whereas transports from Germany and Vienna were designated by Roman numerals. Although there was no transport JIV, the designation indicates that it would have arrived in 1943.

official had been arrested for stealing from the Post Office.[45] However, the Supreme Court's sentence was passed in complete secrecy and without any publicity.

The Creator had become so much at one with His chosen role as Aaron Gottesmann that He felt all the bitterness of his fate. It was not

---

45 Beginning in September 1942, prisoners were permitted to send postcards once every few months and to receive restricted types of packages, if they still had anyone in the free world to whom they could turn. The packages were examined in the post office for "contraband" (cigarettes, money, alcoholic beverages, etc.) and part of their contents would often be stolen by the postal workers examining them.

until He had to listen to Pentlička's ironic comments about how God could bear to watch what was going on, that He began to realize His divine nature and how he ought to be judging what He saw. He himself was unjustly sentenced; He saw how some were hungry and others had overstuffed bellies; He saw the desperation and fears of those who tried to act justly; He felt the helpless suffering of the humiliated and the wounded, and He felt it was unjust that He should be blamed, He who did all things for the best. No wonder that people no longer believed in Him, and if they did, then only because they feared His retribution. Oh, how difficult the task of the Almighty, when His will was distorted by so many unworthy creatures He Himself had put in charge of their suffering brethren.

He was thinking thus sadly as lunch time approached. He searched for his food ration card,[46] turning over all his things, and then noticed an

---

46 Food distribution was done by a monthly food ration card with squares for each day. One functionary with scissors stood near the distribution point and cut away that day's square from each person's card before s/he could approach the distribution counter.

envelope under his mattress. When he looked inside he was amazed: a hundred mark bill. Did one of his kinder fellows want to show sympathy in this way? How touching! If only he could find out who had thus helped him, and give back this financial assistance. For the moment he left the envelope where it lay, and hurried to get his midday meal.

Lunch that day was hirse [millet gruel], something that divided ghetto opinion like Zionism, or when the war would end. Aaron Gottesmann found hirse so good that he went up for a second helping.[47] In the queue he first heard of the berušky (ladybugs),[48] and he realized that their presence made people nervous. He had thought that ladybugs were harmless insects, but it seemed that they were not so harmless, if everybody was afraid of them. It must have been the subject of animated discussion in the room, because tension lay heavy in the air.

This did not prevent Aaron Gottesmann from falling asleep, however, and it was late afternoon before he woke. He would have slept on, but a buzz of excitement woke him. It was pleasurable excitement this time, and he understood that the ladybugs had left the building without coming into their room at all. He remembered the envelope—who could have been so generous? Pentlička? Or one of the others? Perhaps there would be some mark on the envelope that would help him to find out. Now what did this mean? The envelope had disappeared. He decided

---

47 Nachschub in ghetto slang. Second portions were distributed only if something remained in the vat after everyone had received a portion.
48 An untranslatable pun on the Czech word for ladybug, beruška. In Czech, the first syllables, "beru", means I take, I steal, which is exactly what those uniformed German women, who were sent by the SS to control the inmates, did. They would search the premises for "contraband" and steal whatever suited them.

to tell the whole story to Mr. Pentlička, who was just marking his linen. He watched the man's face intently, hoping to see some sign of his worthiness. First Pentlička looked him long in the eye, his mouth grew stern, and then he looked down, shaking his head, and said kindly: "Anyone can see you're a greenhorn. Don't you know that Jews are not allowed to have money? Only today they arrested two old women in this very house, because the ladybugs found a handful of pennies in their belongings.

So you see, you don't have to guess much which of us could have given you money, OK?"

"So that's how it is," Aaron Gottesmann sighed heavily and sat deep in thought for some time.

They had all gone to sleep that evening when the order came for

Blocksperre[49] [curfew] next morning; nobody was to leave the house.

What was going to happen this time? Nothing pleasant. Men in white, calling themselves doctors and armed with magnifying glasses, went from house to house and room to room, examining all the inmates one by one, looking for lice.

Terezín and lice—two things as inseparable as Pardubice and its gingerbread, or Olomouc and its cheese. The first lice to appear in Terezín—they were said to have come from Vienna—caused an uproar. People held their breath and made a wide detour around the infested spot, and gazed horror-stricken at the bonfires in the courtyards, consuming mattresses, articles of clothing and even someone's entire baggage. In those days, lice were something mysterious, almost mystical. Much had changed since then; a complete delousing department had been set up and hundreds of people found employment there, as reputable a job as that of Kaninchenhaarschererei, Kriegsbeschädigten und Körperbehinderten-Fürsorge, or Glimmerbrechen.[50] They proudly wrote Entwesung [delousing][51] in big letters over their door, and flung themselves into the louse war wholeheartedly and systematically. They fought with leaflets, with lectures, with regulations and prohibitions—

---

49   Lockdown of an apartment block.
50   Rabbit shearing, welfare for war victims and for the handicapped, and splitting mica, respectively. Raising rabbits for hair was ordered by the SS. Splitting mica, "Glimmer" in ghetto language (Glimmerspalten was the official term), was done with a sharp knife by women seated on stools. The mica was divided into thin leaves for the Luftwaffe, and it saved the lives of hundreds of women because their work was needed until the ghetto was liberated.
51   This was a special Nazi term. *Wesen* implies production, whereas the prefix *ent* implies the end of the activity—killing. Outside the camps, the Nazis used the standard German word *Desinfektion* for this.

and occasionally with Lysol. It was no longer considered a disgrace to be infested with lice in Terezín. You caught them like you caught a cold, without knowing where and when.

There were always surprises; those you would least expect, often turned out to be harboring the creatures. That was what happened this time. Nobody in the room had any idea that there was anything wrong, and there was the doctor, peeping under one collar after another and lo and behold! "Schwester, schreiben Sie auf,"[52] and three more names were added to the list: Herzfeld, Kraus and Gottesmann. It could just as well have been any of the others, and what would they have felt like if they'd been pushed away, backs turned on them, things moved out of their reach as though it was the plague they had contracted, the way they treated those three? And although there was a certain bond between the victims, each withdrew into himself and felt humiliated as never before. That night, none of the three slept, thinking with terror of what was going to happen the next day.

Aaron Gottesmann obeyed the Hausältester's orders and carried all his possessions into the courtyard to join the pile of bundles and cases waiting to be taken away. He thought of taking this opportunity to end his earthly pilgrimage, but changed his mind, partly out of curiosity to see what was in store for him, and partly because he did not want to risk taking his lice back to Heaven with him.

Early next morning they were hurried out into the courtyard where quite a few others were already waiting, most of them elderly, skinny and shivering from cold. After being lined up and having their names

---

[52] "Nurse, write it down." The sentence is in German in the original Czech manuscript.

read out, which took some time, they were marched along down the middle of the road; the sick and handicapped were pushed along in an old-fashioned hearse — the universal vehicle for all loads, but never used for carrying corpses. Those were treated differently. As the group marched along, they saw a load of that sort of goods. From a distance it looked like a heap of vanilla rakvičky [coffin-shaped cakes], like the ones we used to see at confectioners in bygone days; there were twenty-seven of them, in three layers. The load aroused no more interest than a pile of panels being taken to insulate the attics that had to be used for living quarters when there was no more room anywhere else.

Our sad procession was making its way for the Jägrovka,[53] a grim place hollowed into the ground, with a layer of earth for a roof. The poor creatures were taken into a dark room where a stove gave off practically no heat; there they had to strip and tie their clothes into a bundle for the gas chamber.[54] Then came what they all feared most — the humiliating process of being shaved. The doctors may have been right, but the ordinary layman will never believe that for one single louse resting on a collar for a moment, it was necessary to be so shamefully marked for the world to see, to be plucked ruthlessly like a chicken, and to be robbed of one's only glory, one's pride, part of one's self.[55] Hair and whiskers gone, it was the turn of the rest of the body, where not a

---

53 The "Hunter's Barrack," the slang name for one of the barracks.
54 This gas chamber was used only for disinfection. The ghetto residents were unaware of gas chambers used to murder human beings.
55 This drastic treatment was undertaken in order to deal with the high death rate that resulted from malnutrition. The SS was uninterested in the death rate, until body lice and the resultant cases of spotted typhus were discovered. The SS feared that the disease might spread to the "Aryans" living nearby.

hair was allowed to remain. Then they were scrubbed in a bath, with rough scrubbing brushes, washed in stinking Lysol and then washed once more.

"Things wouldn't be so bad," an old man said, shivering with cold as they waited endlessly for their deloused clothes to be brought back, their bellies rumbling from hunger.

"Things wouldn't be so bad if they did not behave so savagely. They're like hounds. Why do they yell at us and treat us worse than cattle? They're no better than we; they're Jews just like us. That's the saddest thing of all, that we've created our own Hell here. Everything would be bearable if the handlers weren't such savage beasts. Our bellies might rumble even worse than now, but the same would apply to everybody. We could sleep on the bare ground, all of us the same and none better off than the rest. If there was as much justice as in the trenches, when one gets hit and the other is missed, we'd all suffer together like brothers; there'd be something noble in our suffering. But what you see around you here fills every decent man with loathing. A few hundred living in a comfort they never knew before, while thousands of poor beggars are robbed of the little they're supposed to get; thousands crowded into

miserable bare rooms so that any Wichtigmacher[56] who wishes can have a room to himself, like those women I don't want to mention, who keep on good terms with their bosses. Let me tell you, gentlemen ..."

"Telling us," those in his proximity interrupted the old man as his indignation rose, "every child here knows everything you are saying. It's all the fault of the administration for letting this happen, indeed they encourage it. My son came to see me the other day, gentlemen, and guessed at once that there must be something wrong. He doesn't have time to waste going about visiting; he's been working himself to death

56 A person who sets himself up as someone important.

in the head office for two years now. So I asked cautiously: 'Anything wrong, Pavel?' And he looked at me sadly, then dropped his eyes and all at once he burst out:

'Dad, I can't go on any longer. I'm fed up to the teeth with it all. If you saw what was going on, like I do now, you'd agree with me.'

I felt sorry for him and said, 'Well, give up the job; you don't get much out of it anyway.' 'It's not the job, Dad, you don't get me. I don't mind the work and I can't imagine not working. I'll go on with it as I've been doing, so long as there are a few decent people left in Terezín. How many do you think there are? That's not what I expected our community to be like. I was foolish enough to believe we were better than other people, and that we'd be able to run our own model state properly and make our people happy. Even discounting all the outside influences, I know now that it's not true. And our representatives are the worst of all—loud-mouthed about together bearing our fate, and in reality looking for every chance to better themselves and win the favor of those above them. The methods they use to get there are more than shameful, and I've told them so often enough. They don't like me for it. Our enemies are right: rascals and scoundrels. I'm not swearing at them, I'm just unhappy to have lost the last thing I had—faith in mankind and a better world.'

"Gentlemen, I've never before seen my son weep, and I felt like weeping with him. He's all I've got and I'm proud of him." Then he added with a sad smile: "He won't be proud of a lousy old father when he hears about it."

"You mean deloused, don't you?" someone else said. "We can go back to the others as soon as they give us our clothes back."

They got their clothes back, but don't ask what they looked like. A fortnight in the šlojs wouldn't have ruined things like that couple of hours in the gas chamber. Nevertheless, they all dressed hurriedly, impatient to leave the scene of their humiliation.

Aaron Gottesmann had not escaped the barber's scissors and razor. It depressed him, and he was angry with himself for the mess he looked. However, he'd seen another facet of life in Terezín and heard interesting talk. He was so taken with what that father had said about his son, that he wanted to get to know the young man. He decided to ask the old man what his son's name was, and where he could be found.

Back in their room, the deloused men were paid no attention and saved from the humiliating embarrassment they had feared, thanks to a new excitement that was running wild throughout the town. There was something grave and heavy in the air. It slowly dawned on Aaron Gottesmann that two crazy fellows did not like the ghetto—or, as it was lately called, the "Jewish Self-Administration"[57]—for whatever reason, and had run away in the night. This shocking act provoked the dire indignation of the responsible office,[58] and reprisals were immediate. Ausgehsperre was imposed—nobody was to leave their rooms except for official purposes; lights were forbidden, electric or otherwise; no amusement or entertainment, or any other such bright ideas, were permitted. And even harsher measures would be taken if anything of the

---

57 As part of the project to beautify the ghetto in preparation for the visit of the International Committee of the Red Cross, which took place in June 1944, the ghetto's name was changed to Jüdisches Selbstverwaltungsgebiet – Jewish Self-Administration Region.

58 The author was careful not to name the responsible office—the SS—even in a private document meant only for his immediate family.

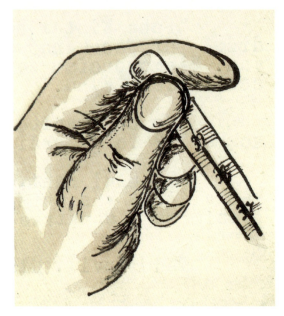
sort happened again. The commandant of the ghetto certainly had no idea that Mr. Reich would go hungry if he couldn't visit his wife in the Dresden barracks for his daily potato soup (the lady was employed there to peel potatoes); that thousands of mothers would not be able to see their children in the children's barracks where typhus and scarlet fever were raging just then; that life in the dark meant drowning in dirt and lice, breaking limbs on dark stairways, not finding the saving bottle of drops when a heart attack came on. Or did he know, and such amusing possibilities were what made him take those measures?

It was doubly unpleasant for Aaron Gottesmann, for he had made up his mind to leave now that he had seen the joys and sorrows of his Chosen People—to go as soon as possible. But he did not want to be the cause of another catastrophe, for his departure would be seen as an escape. How could he solve this dilemma? He could not go on waiting forever, and there was certainly trouble in Heaven by now because he had not returned. True, once or twice a year he would slip away for a while, but he had never, never been away for so long. There would perhaps be no way out except to die like any mortal, be buried and struck off the register. Really, that was the only way. And so he undressed and lay down, shivered with fever and decided to have pneumonia.

It worked. There was nothing strange about it. Mr. Pentlička diagnosed the trouble like an experienced nurse and sent for the doctor. The doctor found a 39°C fever but was in no hurry, next day would show whether it was jaundice, but personally he suspected typhus.

As he lay there, Aaron Gottesmann's head was spinning with all he had heard and seen in Terezín, and he was getting ready for the meeting he would convene as soon as he got back, and all he would have to tell them. A lot of things would have to change. To begin with, that war would have to stop. But first He would have to decide what was to be done with His Chosen People. Should He lead them back to the Promised Land, or should He leave them scattered in the Diaspora?

A pity about the Ausgehsperre; he would have liked to find that young man, now what was his name again? Pavel that was it, Pavel Winter, a lawyer by profession. He had certainly had plenty of experience and would be able to explain why things were going so wrong in this Jewish community.

It was quite dark in the room; now and again a shadow could be seen moving about. Since Aaron Gottesmann had a real fever, they sent for the doctor again. He still wouldn't say what was wrong, but that next morning he'd be taken to the Vrchlabí barrack [infirmary].[59] He wrote a prescription, but they didn't have that drug in the pharmacy. Couldn't Mr. Gottesmann get hold of it himself? "You know how it is," with

---

59 This was the Czech name of a town that the Germans called Hohenelbe. This barrack housed the main infirmary.

a shrug, "there are many people sick but not enough medicine." Mr. Pentlička knew of a woman who worked in a doctor's office and once got him some Cybasol [anti-viral medication] for a thousand crowns, not expensive at that. Only how could he get to her when nobody was allowed on the streets?

A stranger came into the room, asking for Mr. Winter. "He's in the corner over there, but mind your way, there's a bucket there. Don't knock it over."

"What do you want me for?" Mr. Winter sounded scared.

"Don't be afraid, Mr. Winter, I'd rather be knocked about than have such bad news to tell. The Almighty has found it good to summon your son to Him."

"You're crazy, you mean my Pavel? There must be a mistake somewhere."

"I'm afraid there's no mistake. We worked together in the same office, and I know you by sight. Please accept my condolences. I know it's a terrible blow, but ..." and his voice broke.

"My God, what happened? I'll never get over this," Mr. Winter groaned and fell back on his bunk.

"Mr. Winter, calm yourself! Mr. Winter, there's no point! Mr. Winter, you've got yourself to think of!" his neighbors cried one above the other as they stumbled in the dark to grip his hand.

"Tell me what happened, please," the despairing father sobbed.

"It was so sudden, I don't know how to explain it. About a week ago he started acting very strange, left his work and came to see you, I think. Next day he was normal again. Today he had another attack; he started shouting at us, which he normally would never do. He called us thieves and murderers and he slapped the boss's face. Then he jumped out of the window, and he was dead before we got to him. It was such a strange and terrible scene; we were petrified."

"You said that the Almighty found it good, eh? Just like that. And it had to be my son. I'll have an account to settle with the Almighty; thank you, and forgive me; I know you're not to blame. Could I ask you to go and tell my wife? I'll tell you where she lives—because I can't go myself, with the curfew."

Aaron Gottesmann's heart was thumping as he listened in, and sweated profusely.

What a tragedy he had caused with his lack of prudence. It could not be undone, but he would have to do something for poor old Winter. Perhaps he could be given a job in the food depot, cutting up margarine or something ...

Early next morning two Krankenträger [orderlies] came looking for the patient to take to the typhus ward, much to Aaron Gottesmann's surprise. It was no good protesting that he had pneumonia; the orders read "typhus" and that was that. Well, he thought to himself, it doesn't really matter, since I want to die anyway, and maybe it will be quicker this way.

The wards with their more or less clean beds were not nearly as terrifying as the posters hanging in the barracks,[60] and there was more talk of typhus outside than here where men were just lying, getting weaker and hungrier—and of course, dying. So long as Death came

---

60 These were posters meant to promote the fight against lice.

for its victims in reasonable numbers, you bit your lip and watched the figures and the graphs, but the day Death practically wiped out the girls' home, the doctors put their heads together and began to take more severe measures.

"I know a family," a patient near Aaron Gottesmann said, "that paid a dreadful price for typhus—the wife worked in the kitchen and after she got over typhus they wouldn't take her back in case she was carrying the bacillus. It was a catastrophe for the family; the food she'd been taking home sustained her husband, a young daughter, her mother and two brothers with their wives; often she'd hand round potatoes in the barracks of an evening, not to let them spoil overnight. Besides that, she had special ration coupons, and she'd use them to pay her bills, as if they were checks. A week's worth to the cobbler for mending her shoes, a fortnight's to the dressmaker for making a dress, or a lemprček,[61] and so on. Now they're all in a real mess."

"It's not such a good thing anymore; the Wipo[62] are now closely controlling everything. A cook was sacked on the spot for trying to smuggle out a single dumpling[63] for his kids."

"He must have been a fool. Nobody with their wits about them has to go hungry in Terezín, let me tell you. Of course what they give us wouldn't keep you alive for a month, that's why everybody does his best

---

61 The word is a Czech colloquialism for lumberjack and refers also to the short, warm coat worn by lumberjacks.
62 Wirtschaftspolizei, the economic police, whose main job was to prevent theft.
63 Knedlík are Czech dumplings made of flour and yeast with a bit of sweet sauce on top. For the inmates, this was a treat. Potatoes were served once a week.

to get hold of somebody else's. Just imagine the cunning of a thirteen-year-old girl who was supposed to bring her urine to the doctor and instead sold her Friday ration of margarine and sugar to her friend

who had something wrong with her liver, for the friend's urine and of course to get her diet."[64]

The rest of the conversation was lost on Aaron Gottesmann, floating in a confused murmur far, far away. He just heard the doctor stop by his bed and say to the nurse: "Another piece of awful work — a clear case of pneumonia and they send him in here! What can I do? Not that it matters; he won't last longer than this evening, anyway."

The doctor moved on and the nurse came to sit by Aaron Gottesmann's bed, taking his hand gently and then dropping it in disappointment, grumbling: "A bachelor, by the look of him, not even a ring ..."

Twice a day, morning and afternoon, a crowd of mourners waits in the long, chilly, vaulted room badly lit by a single bulb, and each takes his stand by one of the coffins arranged in two rows, one on top of the other. A ticket with Aaron Gottesmann's name on it was pinned to one of them. A rabbi from some foreign land[65] read thirty names in ceremonial

---

64 Surprisingly, Terezín cooked for twelve special diets, such as for hepatitis, kidney disease, diabetes, and other illnesses. Ghetto inmates received 20 grams each of margarine and sugar every three days, and sometimes a pinkish spread called paštika made of an unknown substance.

65 The reference is probably to a German or Austrian rabbi, rather than a Czech rabbi.

sing-song, praying for the dead brothers and sisters, and giving two of them special mention. Aaron Gottesmann was not one of them; he had not been one of the prominenten[66] and had no right to beg a privileged place in Heaven, he had never held office in the Jewish community, had never said Shalom[67] in greeting. He was just an ordinary ghetto inmate, the sort nobody took any trouble over, and whose only right was the right to die.

A cart was waiting outside in the street, drawn by a tractor with its engine idling. In their white overalls, the bearers rushed to the coffins, loading them onto the cart while the sing-song voice of prayer rose and fell monotonously. The procession of silent mourners moved off symbolically, fifty feet or so down the road towards the guard post, the sacred frontier between the ghetto and that other world.[68]

For the forty-five thousand men and women forced to spend their days in bitter slavery, everything beyond the gates and the barbed wire seems a pretty fairyland. They know well enough that there, too, human hearts are full of pain and sorrow, but they prefer to forget this. With tears in their eyes they think of the homes they have left, where life was

---

66 The Prominenten, approximately 200 people, were the privileged inmates, such as internationally renowned scientists, former government ministers, or people protected by the Nazi leadership, who lived in slightly better conditions than the other prisoners, and, most importantly, were generally protected from transports to the East.

67 There was a certain measure of animosity between the Czech prisoners and the Zionists, called *šalomáci* (those who say "shalom") in ghetto slang. Czech Jews who were not Zionists claimed that it was enough for a person to say "shalom" in order to receive protection.

68 The Jewish cemetery was outside the fortress walls and was off-limits to the inmates. At first, the dead were buried in the ground. As the death rate rose, a crematorium was built on the cemetery grounds in the summer of 1942, after which the bodies were cremated.

not always easy, and probably won't be easy when they get back there either …

When they get back there!

All the time He spent in Terezín, God did not meet a single soul without hearing those words, words like a confession of faith, like a love song, like a hymn of praise. Few of the twenty-four thousand whose names are already registered as dead ever doubted for a moment that they would once again see the beloved town they came from, their street, their own home. To the last breath they believed it, and yet they were not rewarded. But, as they died, they believed that at least their children would live to see the day when the fate of millions would be changed.

Vitězslav Taussig, Mr. Pentlička, old Mr. Winter and all the rest would go on believing in the face of all the trials sent to them (as they thought) by God.

No, indeed, this was not God's work. He had come to Terezín a few days earlier, called down to Earth by the fervent prayers of Vitězslav Taussig; and here in Terezín He had seen the sufferings of his People. And He saw that it was bad, and it made Him miserable. Now He was hurrying away—see Him over there, disappearing behind the crematorium—hurrying home, to Heaven, to take things properly in hand.

Be patient a little while longer, wait quietly, and you will soon be rewarded. And then forgive Him, please, because He didn't mean it to be like that.

About the Author

Otto Weiss was born in Pardubice in 1898; in his youth he wrote poems and was a talented pianist. But he was drafted to fight in World War I immediately after his matriculation exams that were administered earlier than usual. In the war, he was wounded in his hand and taken prisoner by the Russians. When he returned to Prague he became a bank clerk and was forced to give up piano playing due to his injury, though he obtained some solace by continuing to write poems, especially after the Nazi occupation in March 1939. Before Otto was deported to the Terezín ghetto with his wife and his daughter Helga in 1941, he committed his poems to memory and re-wrote them in the ghetto. Before his expulsion to Auschwitz in October 1944, Otto handed over his poems, together with *And God Saw That It Was Bad*, to a relative who remained behind in the ghetto. This relative hid Otto's literary collection in the Magdeburg barracks, and thus they were saved. The poems were published in Prague in 1998 under the title *Tak bolely hvězdy* (How the Stars Were Hurting). *And God Saw That It Was Bad* appeared in Czech in 1998 and then in German translation four years later.*

---

* Otto Weiss, *Tak bolely hvězdy* (Prague: Sefer, 1998); idem, *Und Gott Sah, daß es schlecht War* (Gottingen: Wallstein, 2002).

Afterword
The Terezín Ghetto — A Matter of Perspective

An objective picture of the Terezín ghetto is simply not possible. Everything is subjective; everything is relative. In the death camps, those who had been inmates in the Terezín ghetto remembered the ghetto fondly, even with longing. After all, in the ghetto they had been together with their families and had been blissfully unaware of the existence of the death factories. In the ghetto, they had still been able to maintain some form of personal hygiene, and hunger had been bothersome but not maddening and deadly; in the ghetto, they had still been able to read books and enjoy some forms of entertainment.

However, even during the stay in the Terezín ghetto there was a chasm between conflicting points of view among the prisoners: elderly people from the Reich and from Vienna were deported there without their families, exhausted and in shock that the Germans had lied when assuring them that they were going to a sanatorium. In the ghetto they had to lie on straw mattresses on the floor of a suffocating attic and were given food that they could not digest at their age. In short, Terezín was the height of suffering to them. By contrast, young people from Bohemia and Moravia had suffered social isolation in the years of Nazi occupation prior to the ghetto when they had been expelled from schools and suffered countless restrictions in their daily lives. Now, they actually breathed more freely in the ghetto. They lived in children's homes with their peers, without parental imperatives; they studied, they experienced their first loves, worked in vegetable gardens, acquired vocations, held parties, prepared plays. Thus, despite the malnourishment and high rate of morbidity, the Terezín ghetto was something of a positive experience for the youth—until they were sent to their deaths in the extermination camps.

The way the middle-aged people coped with ghetto conditions depended on several factors: their basic personalities, their emotional and physical resilience, luck, their worldviews, and their overall ability to overcome obstacles. Most of the Czech Jews—including the author of *And God Saw That It Was Bad*—were descendents of nationals of the Austro-Hungarian monarchy. They had grown up in an organized and law-abiding world with enduring customs, and even though most were secular or semi-secular, they carried with them a sense of moral superiority towards non-Jews—perhaps because of persecution suffered in the past. The equal rights they had enjoyed in the Czechoslovakian Republic had planted in them a basic belief in justice and the rule of law. From March 1939, these laws had been trampled by the Nazi occupier. Jewish possessions had been stolen, and the Jews had lost their sources of livelihood. They were crushed under hundreds of prohibitions, yet their longing for justice and equity in this world remained alive.

Many went to the Terezín ghetto under the illusion that they were to reside temporarily in an organized Jewish city until the world would return to normal. They were unprepared and shocked at the reality that greeted them: terrible crowding, the need to improvise basic necessities, and the steady flow of transports entering and exiting the ghetto to an unknown destination in the East. Their frustrations were directed at the

Jewish leadership, despite the fact that the leaders were subject to the authority of the SS exactly like the rest of the ghetto's inhabitants. The SS commandant determined the extent of the population density in the ghetto, the prohibitions on going out into the street, the limitations on turning on lights. It was the SS that confiscated most of the baggage and possessions of the new inmates in the sorting area that was nicknamed the *šlojs* (*Schleuse*; sluice), or floodgate. Thus the word *šlojs* became synonymous with thievery in the ghetto vernacular.

The original Czech edition of *And God Saw That It Was Bad* includes hundreds of expressions in ghetto slang, most of them in German with a Czech dialect. Some examples are *Zícha* or *Sieche* for a terminally ill person; *Geťák* or *Ghettowache* for Jewish policeman; *Kripouš* or *Kriminalpolizei* for criminal police; *Tunka* or *Tunke* for sauce; *Klodienst* for public lavatory service; *AK*, short for *Aufbaukommando*, which referred to the unit of Jews that had set up the ghetto and who for a limited time period enjoyed immunity from transport to the East. The existence of this Terezín slang is testimony to the extent to which its inmates became habituated to ghetto reality.

In the reality of *And God Saw That It Was Bad*, the authority of the Nazi regime is not felt. The SS rulers appear only infrequently within the ghetto itself. Instead, they cunningly transmit their daily orders and decrees via the Jewish representatives, mainly the Jewish Elder or his deputy. Thus, the inmates turned their bitterness, anger and hatred inwards, towards themselves—as had often been the custom of the Jews for generations—as well as towards their Jewish leadership. Otto Weiss and other Jews like him who considered themselves Czechs of the Mosaic Faith were especially hostile towards the Zionists (called *Šalomáci*, or those who say Shalom) who were the leading figures in the ghetto's leadership during its early period. Ironically, the Zionists were under the illusion that the Terezín ghetto would serve as an asylum for Jews from the Protectorate of Bohemia and Moravia until the end of the war. Thus, they demanded control of those departments that seemed important to them for their anticipated future in Eretz Israel: the Labor Department, the Youth Department, and the Health Department. Meanwhile, the economic departments that wielded the true clout were left to those Czech Jews who were non-Zionists.

True, each member of the Council of Elders—whether Zionist or not—had the right to protect thirty members of his family and friends from transport to the unknown, at least initially. Eventually they, too, were swallowed up. But it was the SS headquarters that determined the number of transports to the East and the number of Jews in each transport—whether a thousand, two thousand, or five thousand people. They also determined the make-up of each transport: whether Jews from the Protectorate area, or from the Reich; whether of working age or elderly—all these orders came from the local SS command according to orders received from Berlin and Prague. For a time, the heads of departments and the directors of the factories were able to protect vital workers, but eventually these workers, too, were sent to the death camps.

It is not surprising that there were mishaps, shortcomings, and arbitrariness in the ghetto. What is amazing is that some kind of order was preserved in that fortified city, which was originally built for 3,500 inhabitants and an equal number of soldiers and now was packed with

50,000 or more prisoners. Every person was assigned a corner to sleep in and received food coupons. The public soup kitchens provided daily food—however meager—to the entire ghetto population, and everyone who was capable of working received medical care, in spite of the shortage of medicine.

True, much was stolen in the ghetto from the public goods, mainly food, and this was done by those who had access thereto—the transport people, the cooks and bakers, those who distributed the food, the storehouse workers, and the women who peeled the potatoes. However, there were relatively few episodes of thievery among the inmates themselves. There was, nonetheless, favoritism in obtaining "lucrative" work assignments (with access to additional food) and in getting sleeping spaces in which one could breathe a bit more freely. While the members of the ghetto's leadership lived with their families in separate, one-room barracks, and in exceptional cases even received two rooms, this was far from the luxurious conditions attributed to them by the average inmates, who were crowded by the hundreds in barrack dormitories and by the dozens in each room of the houses. A short time after the establishment of the ghetto, those Jews who had high-level leadership positions were sent by the SS to live in the Magdeburg barracks, which was also the site of the administration. But even if those "privileged" ones had resided with all rest of the inmates—and Weiss talks only about a few hundred "privileged" people—it would not have alleviated the terrible crowding of the tens of thousands.

True, the Jewish policemen strutted around the ghetto as authorities; sometimes they shouted, often they were arrogant, but they never hit or abused the others. Weiss, however, judges the policemen by the high standards of his past life and renders their rude behavior towards the weak elements in the ghetto as cruelty. And despite the terrible crowding, there were no cases of murder or of inflicting injuries among the inmates. There were no rapes and no physical violence.

Compared to the darkness of the death camps in Poland and the concentration camps in Germany to which they were later deported, the former inmates of Terezín saw in the ghetto a half-full cup. However, Otto Weiss judged his ghetto existence on Czechoslovakian soil according to the ideals of yesteryear—and even then, there was an enormous gap between the people of means and the beggars. But now, in the Terezín ghetto, he saw only the half-empty cup, the God who had failed him.

Linguistic Issues

The ghetto was run in the German language. Some of the terms used in the ghetto were determined by the SS commandant, while some were set by the Jewish leaders. The Czechoslovakian Jews had also used German vocabulary in their daily life, sometimes modifying the terms to the Czech language. Since Otto Weiss inserted ghetto-specific German terms into his Czech text, such German terms have been retained here as well, in order to demonstrate the inmates' conformity to the German rules and routines that were imposed upon them. Each term is explained.

Ruth Bondy

Afterword translated from the Hebrew by Sandy Bloom